SPEED OF WINTER

ANDY COOMBS   SARAH SCHO

Index

Do it again

"No, no, NO! Do it again."

Nora sighed, stretched her fingers, and started from the beginning.

"No! You're not concentrating!" Her father was cross.

"I am!"

"No, you're not. Your fingers should stroke the keys. Feel the music. When you play the piano becomes part of you."

Nora tried again.

"No! Come on Nora, this is an easy piece of music."

"It may be for you, you're a concert pianist."

"It is for anybody!"

"Maybe if you let me play on your piano, I would be better."

"No. Until you know how to respect the music you must practice on this one."

In Nora's home there were two pianos. The one her father played on – a beautiful grand piano made from the best golden spruce wood – and the one she played on. An old, rotten plywood thing that Nora hated.

"I'm tired now. I've been practicing for an hour already."

"And if you want to be a good pianist like me, you need to practice for two hours every day."

"Maybe I will never be like you. Maybe I don't have it in me. The music."

Her father's eyes flashed angrily. *"Music is in everybody. You need to work to get it out. You're just being lazy!"*

"No, I'm not! I'm trying! You just expect too much of me."

"Of course I don't. Stop being silly. I love you. I just want you to be the best that you can be."

"Yeah," said Nora quietly, *"but what if my best isn't enough for you?"*

Her father sighed. *"Ok, that's enough. Come on. Off to bed."*

"Sorry Dad." Nora looked at her father's face. His eyes. His mouth. She remembered when that serious face used to break into smiles; grins that lit the whole room and made you feel special. Made you feel on the inside of a secret.

He pinched the bridge of his nose. *"You're tired. We'll try again tomorrow."*

2

Sweet harmonies

Nora lay in bed and waited. It was cold and dark outside, but the winter moon spread a white light through her window. The old oak tree outside moved gently in the wind – its branches playing with the moonlight, making shadows that danced and stretched on her ceiling.

She knew her father just wanted the best for her, but sometimes he expected too much. Nora's mother had also been a musician. She had played the flute beautifully. That is how Nora's parents had met – playing in a world class orchestra. But when her mother died a few years ago, her father had locked the flute in a glass cupboard.

Nora made pictures with her mind in the moving branch shadows. Her father was right, she was tired, but she wanted to wait. To wait for her father to play. Every evening, after Nora had gone to bed, he would play music that filled the house.

She heard the sound of the grand piano lid being opened. She held her breath. And then the music started. Moonlight Sonata. Her favorite. So sad. So beautiful. The notes drifted into her room and into her mind. Like cool rain falling on hot desert sands. Was her father, right? Did she have music like this within her – just waiting to come out? She didn't think so.

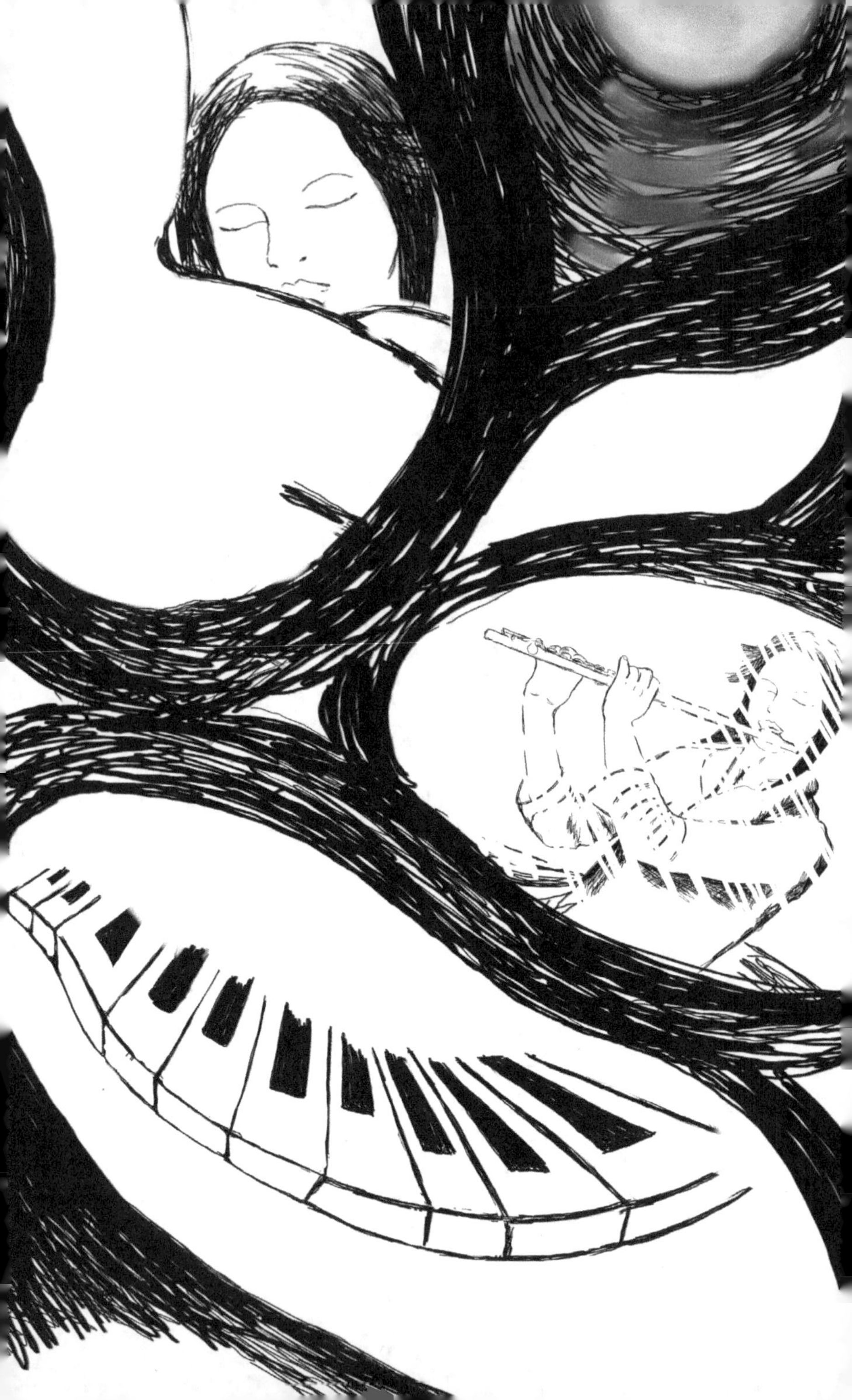

Nora closed her eyes and allowed the sound to take her into her thoughts. She saw her mother and father dancing in the living room. Her mother's head on her father's shoulder. Swaying slowly together from side to side. A year ago, these thoughts would have made her cry. But now they filled her with warmth. She smiled and allowed the sweet harmonies to carry her to sleep.

3

Four-thirty in the morning

Nora opened her eyes. She looked at her clock. It was four-thirty in the morning. The room was full of soft orange light. She got up and padded over to the window. The sun had just started to come up. She wasn't tired any more, but it was too early for breakfast. She didn't want to go back to bed. She pulled on her jeans and a t-shirt. She opened the window a crack to see how cold it was. The air made her shiver. So, she pulled on a sweater and a thick pair of socks. She ran softly downstairs and chose her thickest jacket. The front door closed silently behind her.

Her breath made puffs of smoke in the air. Maybe it would snow this winter! That would be fantastic. Snowmen and snowball fights with her friends.

She ran across the road and into the forest. Everything was different this early in the morning. There were no car sounds, only the wind in the trees and a couple of early birds singing to the dawn. It even smelled different – like the night had cleaned away the smells of yesterday making the air crisp and fresh.

She ran through the trees and down to the lake. In the spring she would look for tadpoles and frogs. She might use her fishing net to hook out fish to put in jam jars. In the summer she would swim and jump from the rocks to make splashes as big as she could. But now the first freeze of winter was coming, she could feel it.

There was a thin layer of ice covering the lake, way too thin to walk on but soon after this first freeze and when it was truly cold the little lake was a perfect skating rink. Nora loved the winter! Towards the middle of the small lake was a dark hole where the ice hadn't quite closed over. She picked up a stone and tried to hit the hole. She missed and made another hole with the stone. The sound of the ice cracking was extremely satisfying. She picked up another stone and threw it. Again, she missed. She used a flat stone to skim over the ice. It spun and slid until it nearly reached the other side. She looked around and found a stone almost as big as her hand.

She stretched her arm right back and threw it as hard as she could towards the hole. The stone spun through the air but just as it was about to land in the middle of the hole a hand pushed its way out of the water and caught it. The hand was followed by a long arm, then a head and a body. And legs. An old man dressed in a long green robe rose from the lake. His feet floated a few inches over the ice. Then he bent down and blew on his hand towards the hole he had come from. The hole turned white and then was smooth with ice.

Nora rubbed her eyes. She must still be asleep. People don't rise out of lakes and then float over the water. She looked again. The man was now floating towards her. She took a step back and punched herself hard on the arm. Ouch! It didn't feel like she was asleep. And then the man was standing in front of her. His head to one side as though thinking. He was tall and thin, with night dark skin, long white hair that stuck out everywhere and bright green eyes. Nora took another step back. Should she run? But she didn't feel afraid. The man had a small smile on his lips. Then he said.

"So, you're the one, are you?"

"I'm sorry?" Nora said.

The man tutted. *"You're the one I'm supposed to meet."*

"I don't know. But who are you? And how…" she looked with wide eyes to the frozen lake, *"…did you do that?"*

The man ignored her.

"Are you ready to get started then?" he asked.

"Start what?" Nora shook her head again. Her head felt like it was full of toffee.

"To start learning to do what I do."

Nora shook her head once more. Hard. *"Hold on a minute. I don't know why you're asking all the questions. How did you come out of the lake? How did you float on the water and make the hole cover over with ice? And why,"* she looked him up and down, *"aren't you wet?"*

The man tutted again. *"We don't have time for this. Well, actually we do. But I don't want to. So, come on. Are you ready?"*

"Look," Nora said angrily. *"I'm not ready for anything except for some answers. First of all, who are you?"*

The man looked confused. *"Don't you know?"* he said. *"Isn't it obvious?"*

Nora looked at the tall, thin man with the crazy white hair, dressed in a freaky green robe. *"No, it's not,"* she said.

Then the man took a step towards the nearest tree. He opened his palm and blew on it, like he was blowing a kiss. White sparkles flew from his palm and hit the tree. Immediately lines of ice, like spider webs, ran up the tree and into the branches. Then each branch was white and shining with ice. But it didn't stop there. The ice jumped from tree to tree. Nora turned around slowly, her eyes wide, her mouth open, watching as the ice flew from tree to tree until the whole forest was covered in ice crystals. She turned back to the old man who was looking at her, his bright green eyes dancing.

"So?" he said. *"Do you know who I am now?"*

"Wow!" said Nora. And then said it again. *"Wow!"*

"Yes, yes," said the man impatiently. *"But do you know who I am now?"*

Nora couldn't speak for a moment. It was all too much. Too unreal. She swallowed. *"Some kind of magic snowman thing?"*

"Snow?" said the man gruffly. *"Snow? Bah! Stupid white stuff. No art. Just covers everything in a lump. You really don't know who I am?"* He shook his head sadly. *"No culture these days. What are they learning in schools?"* he continued to mutter.

"So, who are you?" Nora said again.

The old man looked at her with his bright green eyes. *"I, my dear,"* he said with a flourish, *"am the Man of the North. I am the sounds of winter and the father of ice. But the name I like the most is…"* He bowed low and swept his arm around his green robes, *"…Jack Frost."*

4

The kiss of winter

Nora looked at the strange man in front of her, with his strange green clothes.

"Jack Frost! But I thought you were just a story people tell kids."

"And what's wrong with stories?" Jack looked annoyed again.

"Nothing. I mean, well, they're not real, are they?"

"And don't I look real to you?" Jack Frost pulled his robes about himself.

"Well, yes you do. But this is crazy. If you exist, then what about Father Christmas and the Easter Bunny?"

The old man tutted again. *"Now you're just being silly. They're just stories."*

"But you just said stories were ok?" insisted Nora.

"No, I didn't. Or maybe I did. Whatever. Now, enough questions, we have work to do."

"What? I don't understand. What work?"

"The ice. The frost. We need to start the winter."

Nora looked around helplessly. *"But how can I help?"*

"Easy. Watch." And then Jack opened his palm again and blew. But this time the sparkling crystals fell onto Nora. She gasped and the crystals went into her mouth. She felt them cold and bright in her throat and then down until they filled her whole body. She blinked at the crystals in her eyes and wiped them from her nostrils. She felt cold and warm at the same time.

"What was that?" she asked.

"That, my dear, was the kiss of winter." Jack smiled happily. *"Now you can help."*

***

Jack was still holding the stone Nora had thrown in his other hand. *"Try with this first."* He held it out to her.

She took it. And then looked at it. She felt stupid. *"What do I do with this?"*

"You frost it. Just open your hand and blow over the stone. You'll see."

The stone was cold in her hand. She opened her other hand as she had seen Jack do. Then she blew on her palm. Hard. Suddenly the stone was too heavy to hold. She dropped it and it landed on Jack's foot.

"Ouch!" he shrieked and started to hop around. He looked so funny, his green robes flapping everywhere, that Nora started to laugh.

"That hurt!" he said indignantly.

"Sorry," she said and bent down to look at the stone. It looked like a ball of ice. Almost as big as a football.

"Too much," said Jack and sighed.

*"This is an art. I told you. And I am **The Artist**. This isn't snow. Our work is delicate. You have ice inside you now. Learn to use it well. Here."* Jack picked up a twig from the ground. *"Try again."*

This time Nora blew gently. Ice crystals carried on her breath. The twig turned white and frosty. She held it up, seeing how the sunlight made it sparkle.

"Beautiful," she whispered.

Jack took the stick from her and looked at it critically. *"Not really,"* he said. *"You have a lot to learn. And the best way is for you to try on your own. I have a lot to do."*

And suddenly he was floating again. His toes three feet from the ground.

"But… what do you want me to do?" Nora asked desperately.

"Start small. You do your little town and I'll do the rest of the country. We'll meet back here when you're done."

"The whole town? I can't walk that fast."

"Oh yes, I forgot." Jack blew again and the crystals covered Nora's feet. *"Just think up and you'll go up. Flying is much quicker than walking. Try it."*

So, Nora thought *up*. And straight away she rose into the air. In fact, she shot up. Fast.

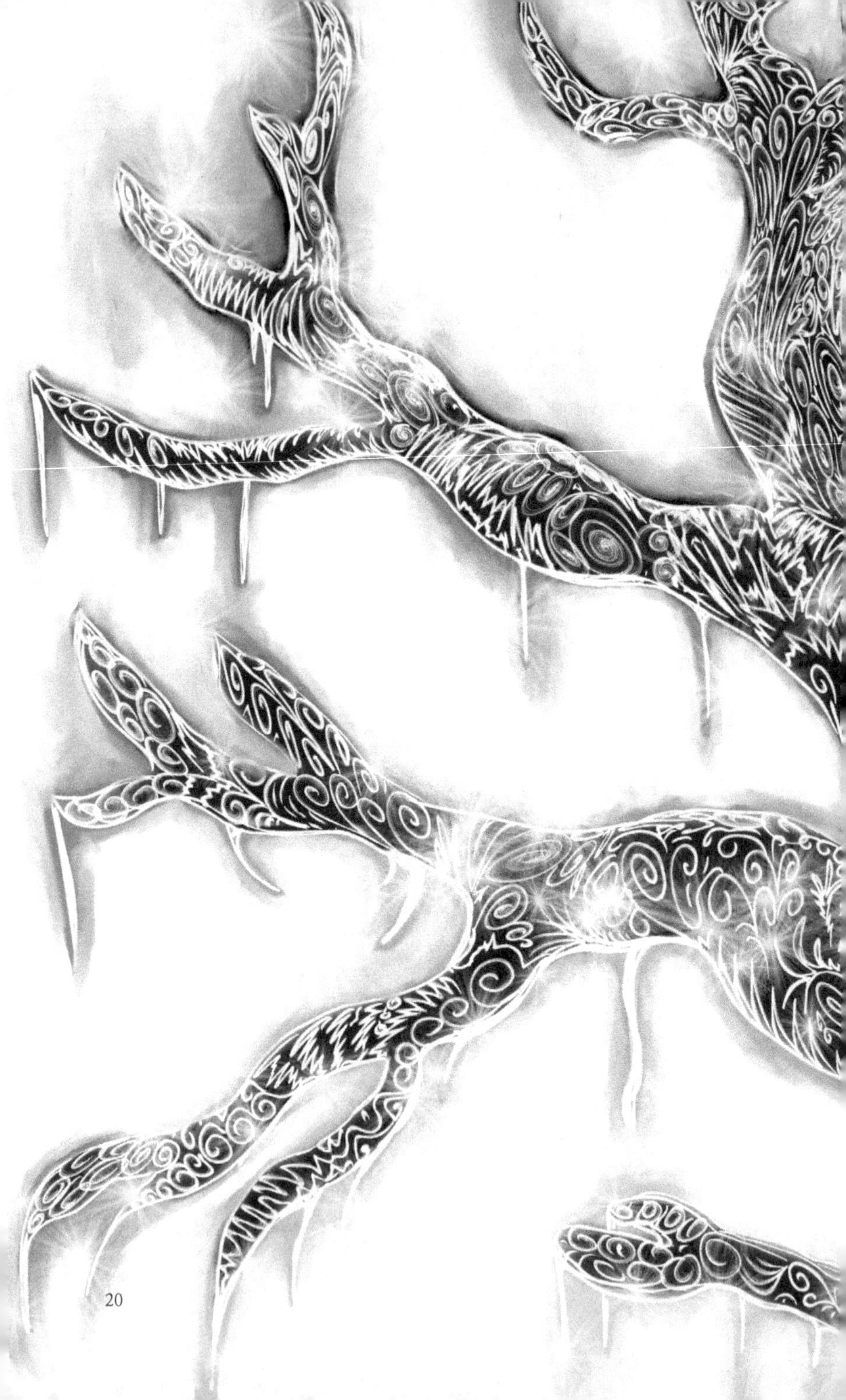

Jack grabbed hold of her foot as she started to zoom past him, screaming. She hovered above him feeling like a kite.

"But not too far," Jack giggled. *"Think up and then stop. And when you want down just think down."*

"I want down. I want down!" screamed Nora.

"So, think it!" Jack yelled at her.

She did. And suddenly Nora tumbled to the ground. *"Ouch!"*

Jack laughed. *"Yes. A lot to practice. I'm off. See you soon. Don't forget. You do the town, I'll take care of everything else."*

He started up, and then stopped.

"You'll know you are finished when you hear the quiet moan of winter," he said cryptically. And then Jack shot up into the sky and was gone.

5

Making ice

Nora rubbed her head. It was sore. She had banged it on the ground. She stood up slowly and looked around. Jack was gone. She felt her head again. Or maybe he had never been here? Maybe she had fallen earlier and bumped her head and now she was just waking up.

There was one way to find out. *Up,* she thought and immediately started to move up. It was real. *Stop!* she thought and stopped, bobbing like a balloon again about three feet from the ground. She laughed out loud.

Up, she thought again and then *stop* when she reached the tops of the trees. She looked over the forest to her house across the road. She imagined Dad inside asleep. Should she go and wake him? Show him what she could do? But no. Jack wanted her to put ice on the town. And if she didn't do it, maybe he would take away her flying. She didn't want that. It was way too much fun.

***

Nora floated down the road. She blew ice onto the puddles and smiled as they froze hard.

She blew ice onto the houses and shops she passed, making ice color the windows white.

She stopped by a low stone wall and blew gently onto a spider's web and watched as the ice moved from strand to strand, making the web glimmer and glisten. She was still nervous about being too high, so she kept close to the ground, taking pleasure from seeing her shadow beneath her rush across the newly white roads.

At the old stone church, she put her lips to the iron door and kissed. She laughed as lines of ice spiraled and played over the metal. The big round door handle froze to the metal. On the colored glass window, the frost crawled and spun into the pictures making the men's beards white and the women's dresses silver.

She was nearly finished. Just the playing field and school. Nora touched her finger to the small river in the field and watched as ice crackled and moved until the river was solid. She ran and skidded across the ice – her boots scratching and kicking up ice flakes and at the last moment she started to fall.

Up, she thought quickly and laughed delightedly as she hovered over the frozen water.

She stood in the middle of the field. She took in a deep breath. She held her palm out and then, spinning slowly, she blew out – steady and strong. Ice powder shot from her mouth and over the grass. Each green blade turned a silvery white. *I'm getting good at this,* she thought proudly.

She paused and closed her eyes. She heard it. Winter's whispered moan. Ice creaking, cold winds playing, leaves crunching and the sound of mud cracking.

She skimmed across the field until she was standing in front of the school building. She could feel the ice in her. Wanting to be out. To cover everything with whiteness. Is this what Dad was talking about? Like music. Something in you that you know can live if you let it.

She closed her eyes and concentrated. She opened her palm slowly in front of her mouth and blew gently. Imagining. Thinking. And when she opened her eyes she laughed with joy. Painted onto the front of the school was an enormous picture of her own face. Her eyes frosty white. Her smiling mouth open, showing silver teeth.

Hah! she thought. *Wait until they see that in the morning. Who's the artist now Jack?*

And then she was finished. She zoomed over the roads back towards the lake. She stopped in front of her house and blew over the garden and walls. Beautiful she thought again. And then flew to the lake.

6

The church spire

Jack was already there. He was sitting on his robe by the frozen water, throwing stones onto the ice as Nora had done before.

He looked up. *"What took you so long?"* he asked.

"I wasn't that long. Maybe an hour or so."

"Actually, you were no time at all," he said. His eyes twinkled.

"What do you mean?"

"I mean, when we do our work, time stops. That's why no people will ever see you. They are all frozen. Not by ice of course. Just time."

"Oh," said Nora simply.

Of course, she thought. *What else could it be?* After flying and breathing out ice – anything seemed possible. Even frozen time.

"And have you – you know – finished as well?"

"Yep. Europe, Asia, the Americas – all done. I'll do home last. On my way back."

"What? You mean the North Pole?"

"No," said Jack and laughed. *"Why would I live there? There's nothing to do. I live in Tanzania. A lovely place right by the foot of Mount Kilimanjaro. I've lived there all my life. Seventy-five years and counting."*

"You're from Tanzania? But I thought, you'd live somewhere magical."

"Trust me. It is magical. Some of the most gorgeous nature in the world. And the best people."

"So, Jack Frost is from Africa?"

"Well, I am. The last one – she was from New Zealand, I think. It was a long time ago."

"You mean there's been more than one?"

Jack tutted again. *"I thought you understood this by now. Being Jack Frost is a job. The old Jack gave it to me about sixty years ago when she got old and now, I'm giving it to you."*

"But why me?"

"Why not you? You were here when I needed someone. I think it just works that away."

"What's it?"

"You know Nature or Earth or whatever. I've never really thought about it. It's just the way it's always been. But now you're my apprentice. A trainee. I train you up this year and for a couple more years and then when I've had enough and want to retire you take over."

"Oh," Nora said again. This was a lot to take in.

"This is a lot to take in," she said.

"Sure. I know. You'll get there. Now, let's go check out your work. Come on."

***

Jack took her hand and together they flew back into the town. Jack nodded approval at the white roads and frosted houses and shops.

"Good job," he said pointing at the school playing field and river. *"Nice work on the grass. Each blade looks great. I can see you have the artist in you."*

"If you like that," Nora laughed, *"wait until you see my school."*

Jack turned and looked. He tutted and put his hand to his mouth. He blew hard and covered Nora's icy self-portrait with new frost.

"Now that is why you need training," he said, *"to learn the rules. Making huge pictures of our own faces is something we don't do."*

"Why not? It was great!" Nora was a bit annoyed that her picture was gone.

"You just don't, ok?" Then Jack looked over her shoulder. *"I can see you've done the church windows and door, but what about the spire?"*

Nora looked up. *"It's so high,"* she said.

"I'm sorry," Jack said in a sarcastic tone, *"I thought I gave you the power of flight. What's the problem?"*

"Heights," said Nora. *"I don't really like them."*

"Well, you have to get over that to do this job." Jack paused a moment. *"You do want to do this job don't you?"* he asked in a worried voice.

"Yes, yes," Nora nodded vigorously. *"Of course I do. Are you crazy? This is amazing!"*

"Well, hold on then." And taking her hand again, Jack shot into the sky.

Jack and Nora landed in the bell tower just under the very top of the church. Jack blew onto the big brass bell and turned it a shining white.

"You do the top of the spire," he said.

Nora looked up and swallowed nervously.

"Go on," Jack said encouragingly. *"You can do it."*

Up thought Nora and floated up. She grabbed hold of the weather cockerel right at the top of the spire and pulled herself up onto it. She was riding it. A gust of wind blew in and the weather cockerel turned slowly.

Like a bucking bronco, thought Nora and holding tight with one hand threw her other into the air as the cockerel spun.

"Woo Hoo!" she yelled. *"Woo Hoo!"*

"Oi! Stop messing about up there. This is work."

Nora looked sheepishly down at Jack's upturned face. But he was grinning.

"Fun isn't it?" he said.

Nora grinned back and blew ice onto the cockerel. Immediately it was ice slippery and she slid off and fell.

"Aiiii!" she screamed and then remembered she could fly.

Stop, she thought and she did. Hovering in the air. The ground a hundred feet below her dangling boots. She flew and rejoined Jack in the bell tower. He was peering up into the wooden rafters.

"Bats!" he said happily. *"I love these little fellas."*

Up in the corners of the rafters were ten or so sleeping bats. Their black fur gleaming – snuggled together for warmth.

Jack raised his hand and blew ever so gently up at them. The ice crystals stuck to their fur and then, as one, all the little bats shivered and shook their wings.

"Are you allowed to do that?" asked Nora laughing.

Jack shrugged. *"I'm Jack Frost,"* he said. *"Who's going to stop me?"*

One of the little balls of fur opened a sleepy eye and glared at Jack.

"How can he look at you?" asked Nora. *"I thought time was frozen."*

"Not for bats," said Jack thoughtfully. *"They see time in a different way to other animals and people. Bats and cats. They're the only two. Strange how that rhymes. Bats and cats. Is that a coincidence I wonder? Hmmm."* He closed his eyes in concentration.

And then taking Nora's hand again, he stepped off the bell tower.

7

Speed

"Where are we going?" yelled Nora into Jack's ear. *"This isn't the way home."*

"No, I have to meet some friends. I want to introduce you to them."

Jack and Nora were flying fast over fields of corn.

Wind whipped into Nora's eyes making her blink cold tears.

"Who?" she yelled again.

"What?" Jack shouted back.

"I said, who are they? Your friends?"

"You'll see. Nice old guys. You'll like them."

Nora closed her eyes and tried to imagine what kind of friends Jack Frost could have.

"Are you ready for this?" Jack yelled again. *"We are about to go really fast. The speed of winter. Just keep thinking go, go, go and hold on to my hand tight. You'll be ok. Are you ready?"*

Nora nodded. And suddenly everything around her blurred. The fields below seemed to stretch out into a thin line. She looked up and the dawn sun smeared into a line that yawned across the sky. And then everything went black, but she could still feel the movement. She held Jack's dry hand tightly.

Go, go, go, she thought. Her mind felt like it was full. Full of speed.

Go, go, go. And then she was still.

Jack's hand was still in hers. She started to move again – this time upwards, through the blackness. And suddenly she was floating above a lake. Above her were stars. It was nighttime. Below her was a frozen lake. In a dark hole, the waters moved and then ice covered the hole. She looked at Jack floating next to her. His hand still in hers.

"Did we just come out of the water?"

"Yep," he said. *"When you move at the speed of winter you always come out of a lake."*

"Why?"

"No idea. But it's cool isn't it?" he grinned again.

Nora nodded in agreement.

"Come on then. My friends will be waiting."

This lake was much bigger than the one in her forest. In fact, Nora couldn't see the edges.

As they skimmed across the white ice of the lake Nora asked, *"Where are we? And why is it dark here?"*

Ahead of them, Nora could see a fire burning. As they sped towards it, she could make out two men, sitting in front of the fire, warming their hands.

8

The Apprentice

Jack landed gracefully four feet or so from the fire. Nora wasn't so graceful and fell into the snow. She spluttered on the snow in her mouth and stood up. Jack was shaking the hand of one of the old men. The man had bright orange hair. The other man wore glasses and was nearly bald. He looked like Nora's Math teacher. The old man whose hand Jack was shaking looked at Nora and laughed.

"So, this is your apprentice Azizi? I see you haven't taught her to land yet."

Jack looked at Nora and laughed too. *"She's ok. She'll learn."*

He took off his green robe and used it like a blanket to sit on. Nora was surprised to see that he was wearing a pair of khaki shorts and a really loud beach shirt with bright reds, yellows and blues. He looked like a tourist.

"Now what do you have for me Fred?" Jack asked the old man with the glasses.

"This," said Fred, producing a small metal flask. *"Chili flavored hot chocolate drink. Made from the finest South American cocoa beans that I personally picked from the top of a mountain. The world's best."* He offered the flask to Jack.

Jack accepted it and took a drink. He smacked his lips. *"Good stuff,"* he said.

Nora looked from one old man to the next. *"Ahem,"* she interrupted, *"I thought you were going to introduce me."*

"Yes, yes," said Jack trying to tut and drink at the same time. It didn't work and he spilt some of the brown liquid onto his green robes. He rubbed at the stain absently.

"This bald old man is Fred, also known as Boreal the North wind. And this red headed old fool is Klaus, also known as Vulcan – the master of fire."

"Who are you calling an old fool, you old fool?" said Klaus and then bowed deeply.

As he straightened, he raised both hands up. Fire jetted out from his palms into the dark starry sky.

Nora jumped back.

"Show off," chuckled Fred and raised his own hand.

Suddenly Klaus was blown from his feet. He landed with a thump on the ground. *"Oi! Watch it!"* he yelled. *"These are new jeans!"*

"Now, now," tutted Jack. *"Stop it both of you. I've come here to introduce my new apprentice to you, and you are showing off like a couple of kids."*

"Yeah, well we've met her now," said Klaus sulkily and sat back down. He took the chocolate drink from Jack's hand.

"So, what's it like Azizi, having an apprentice?" asked Fred.

Nora sat down next to Klaus. He offered her the metal flask. Nora started to take it, but Jack blew ice over her hand.

"No Klaus. She's just an apprentice. She hasn't earned it yet."

"Sorry Azizi," said Klaus.

"Why do they call you Azizi?" asked Nora.

Jack looked at her in surprise. *"Didn't I tell you my name? Jack Frost is my job. It's what I do. Azizi is my name. My real name."*

Nora nodded. She understood.

"Where are your apprentices?" she asked the other men.

"We don't have any yet," said Fred.

"Maybe in a couple of years. But we're not quite so old as Azizi. He's ancient." Klaus laughed at Jack."

"Cheeky!" said Jack but laughed with him.

And then they were quiet. Jack took the flask from Klaus and had another drink and Nora looked up at the stars and then into the fire.

No one is going to believe this, she thought. *But then again, so what?*

"Ok," said Jack, standing up. *"I'm going to take… hold on. I don't actually know your name yet. What is it?"*

"It's Nora," said Nora.

Jack winked. *"For another year or two. Then you'll have a different name."*

"What?" said Nora, not understanding.

"Jack Frost," said Jack. *"You'll be Jack Frost."* He grinned at her.

9

Home

Jack flew her home at the speed of winter. They arrived above her lake. Jack kissed her gently on the cheek and thanked her for her work. Then he left. It was over. For now.

The last thing he said was,

"See you next year!"

Nora couldn't wait.

She went back to bed. As she got under her blankets she looked again at her clock. Jack had been right. It still read four-thirty.

But when she opened her eyes, her room was totally bright, and the clock read seven fifteen. She was starving. She pulled on her clothes again and ran downstairs. Her father was making breakfast. Pancakes and honey. Nora ate three and then asked for another two.

"How did you sleep?" asked her father.

"Fine," she said. *"But I had the strangest dream."*

"Tell me about it," said her father and poured himself a coffee.

So, she did. She told him all about Jack and flying and ice and meeting with Boreal and Vulcan.

"Wow," her father said when she had finished. *"What a dream! Fantastic. Now, can you put that creative energy into playing piano today? Come on let's try."*

***

"No, no, NO! Concentrate."

"I am! This piano is rotten, and it sounds horrible." Nora could already feel herself becoming angry.

"It's not the piano. It's you!"

"No." She banged the keys. *"It's…"* she banged again, *"… NOT!"* She furiously brought both hands down hard on the piano.

She felt something leave her fingers and go into the piano. A coldness. Winter. Suddenly it collapsed in front of her. Her father looked at it with his mouth open.

"Ok," he said slowly. *"That was different. Maybe it was rotten."*

"I told you," she said and smiled sweetly at her father.

"Well, I'll clear this up later. Do you want to keep practicing? I guess now you'll have to use my piano until we can get you another one."

"No," said Nora. *"I think blowing on things is more my talent. Can I have a go with Mom's old flute?"*

Her father looked at her for a long moment. He blinked and wiped his eyes with his sleeve. He took in a breath and let it out.

He looked at the broken piano on the carpet. He nodded and walked over to the cupboard.

Dad fumbled in his pockets but didn't find what he was looking for. He turned and grinned at Nora; the grin she hadn't seen in years; his eyes bright. And then, in a quick movement, he spun and smashed his elbow into the glass cupboard. It shattered, and for a moment it was like time had slowed. Nora watched as each bit of glass spun and dropped like fractured rain to the rug.

Her dad bent down and picked up the flute. He passed it to Nora.

She took in a breath, held it a long time, and felt the winter within her. The ice. The beauty of frost. She was ready.

And then, Nora blew gently into the flute and let her music find its way into the world.

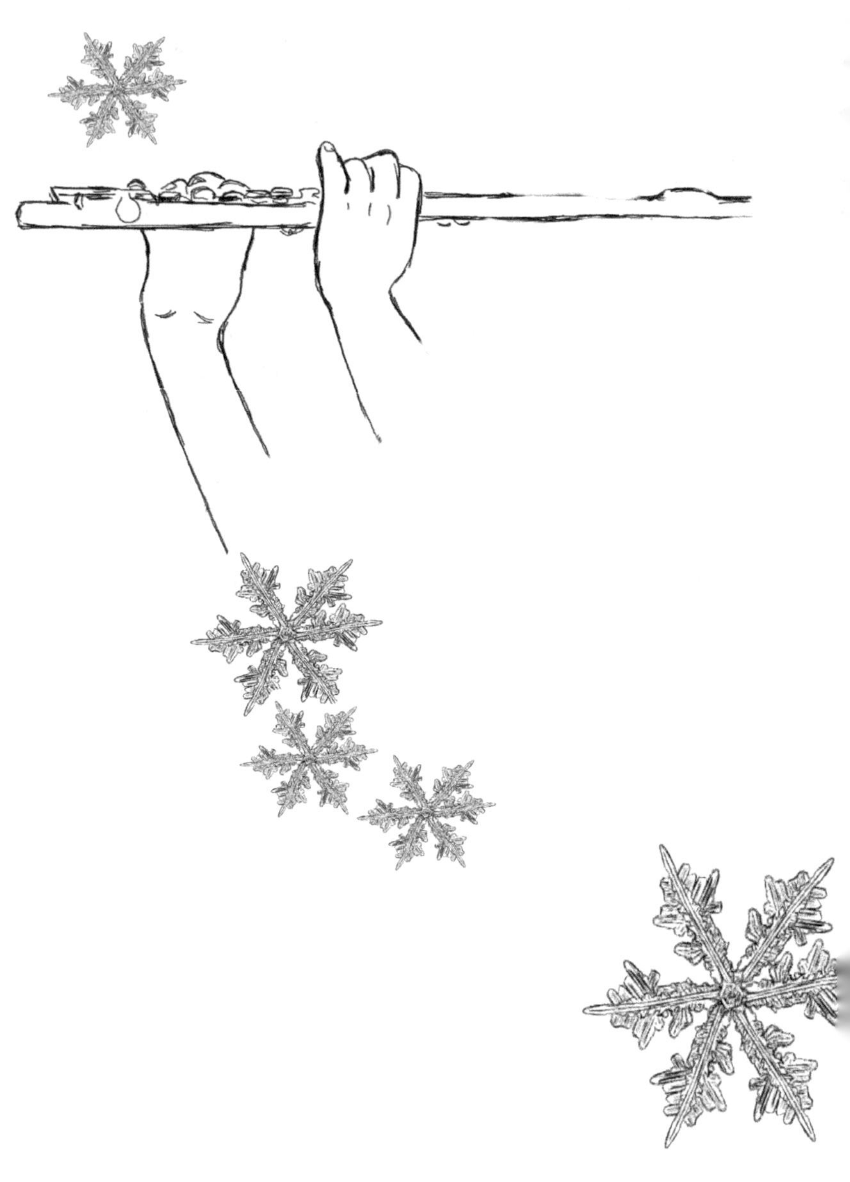

The end.

Andy Coombs

Sarah Scho

Viking Kite stories are written by Swedish-English writers, Andy Coombs and Sarah Scho - both authors and teachers with more than 50 books published and a million books sold in Sweden. Their work and stories have been read and loved by young Swedish minds for more than twenty years and in 2021 are available in translation internationally.

Andy and Sarah live just outside Stockholm in a blue wooden house next to a forest. They live with their tiny black and white dog, Nimly.

Viking Kite stories celebrate life with fun and imagination, encouraging young readers of all ages to see things in new ways.

"Everyone gets to fly the kite."